# A MOUSE, SOME COWS, AND RAIN

## Our Mouse Tale
## A Girl and Some Cows
## The Raindrop Family

# Linda Robinson

www.PHEWpublishing.com

Hardcover: 979-8-9916991-4-3

Paperback: 979-8-9916991-0-5

Kindle also available

Production by Concierge Marketing Inc., www.conciergemarketing.com

Printed in the United States of America

10 9 8 7 6 5 4 3 2 1

To my family, my loved ones, and my Higher Power.

**Hi!**

OUR MOUSE TALE

# OUR MOUSE TALE

December the 12th was a proper cold day.

We were all in the house; there was snow

    on the way.

My ma was quite comfy in her rocking chair,

And Pa was asleep, making growls like a bear.

My brother and I played a game at the table,

And knitting a scarf on the couch was

    Aunt Mabel.

All of a sudden, Ma turned her head—

Was it something Pa did or something we said?

What could it be that could scare Ma the most?

A spirit? A monster? A goblin? A ghost?

It wasn't that someone had stomped on her foot

Or the freezer or fridge going klank, klunk, kerput.

It wasn't the sink running over with bubbles

Or any of those other pesky house troubles.

Then suddenly we saw a flash and a streak,

And we knew right away what made our ma freak.

Aunt Mabel, now sipping her coffee with cream,

Did suddenly scream an old Aunt Mabel scream.

And there in the kitchen, quite snug on the rug,

It wasn't a snake or a bee or a bug,

But the tiniest mouse that you ever did see,

And it made my brother and me squiggle with glee.

Before we could hoot, it zipped under the table

And frightened the coffee right out of Aunt Mabel.

Then faster than we could keep track with our eyes,

It zoomed toward the room with the cleaning supplies.

Ma started to yell, "Land sakes, what was that?"

And Pa growled, "I guess we should let in the cat."

So Pa said to me, "Let the cat in the house,"

To catch what was now our official house mouse.

"An official house mouse," Auntie M said in fear,

"There can't be a mouse living here if I'm here!"

So we all settled down for a cat-and-mouse fight

That surely would take place that December night.

Then at eight on the dot, that mouse reappeared

And started its rampage, just as we feared.

But this time it darted and dashed cross the room,

And Ma tried to shoo it away with a broom.

And my brother and I were whooping and clapping,

But scruffy old cat settled down for some napping.

"Do something!" Ma yelled. "Get that mouse

      out the door!"

Aunt Mabel was screeching, cat stretched on the floor.

Maybe old chunky dog would chase it away,

But the dog's only trick was to sit and to stay.

So thinking as quick and as sly as a fox,

I grabbed something close, like a cereal box.

I plopped it on top of that mouse like a trap,

But it didn't go snap like a snap trap should snap.

Now crushing flakes flew like leaves in the air,

Then settled like dust onto Aunt Mabel's hair.

Well, the wee mouse got scared and jumped up to run,

Jumping so high, landing in Auntie's bun.

"Oh dear!" sighed Mabel. "A mouse for a hat!

What would the ladies from church think of that?"

We looked at old Pa, and Pa gave a soft coo

And said, "Sister Mabel, you'll need some shampoo."

"Get it down!" Auntie wailed, tried bravely to sock it,

But then in a flash, the mouse jumped into my pocket.

That mouse was so cute; I was under its spell—

The whiskers, the nose, that little mouse tail.

And it looked up at me with those pretty brown eyes,

Like an angel, a saint, or a friend in disguise.

"Oh Ma, it's so tiny!" I cried with a pout,

"And it's a cold night; we just can't put him out!

Couldn't we keep little mouse for a pet?

Why, we haven't owned a little mouse yet!"

But Mother quite sternly explained to us all,

"Aunt Mabel will never agree to that call.

Besides, you have birds, a cat, and a dog,

And you've got a rabbit, two fish, and a frog."

But before I could beg or request any more,

Our mouse changed its course and leapt toward
    the front door.

Then I think I saw Auntie's hand turn the knob,

And our rodent escaped with a weave and a bob.

Out through the door where winter was falling,

"Come back, little mouse!" I was secretly calling.

So that is what happened a long time ago

When a tiny gray mouse disappeared in the snow.

Now, 20 years on, I look back to that night—

How that cute little mouse gave us joy and delight.


P.S.


I never told Ma

    —not back then,

        not today—

But our mouse reappeared the 11th of May.

It spent the next months in my comfy ball hat

And it loved going round and around with the cat.

But the strangest thing is, and it gives me a fright,

Our mouse disappeared that next Halloween night.

Then the month of November took October's place,

And old cat lounged around with a grin on its face.

And for many years on, we never did dare

To speak of the rodent in Aunt Mabel's hair.

And oh, did I mention that next Christmas Eve,

Auntie M had a spider crawl way up her sleeve?

A GIRL
AND
SOME COWS

# A GIRL AND SOME COWS

This story is about mean cows in a pasture.

It could have happened last week; it could've

    happened last year.

Well, these cows lived in this pasture, and they

    ate all this grass,

And they stared real mean at anyone who passed.

And there was this girl who wanted to go play

At her friend's house that seemed miles and

    miles away.

But to get there, she must get past those masters

    of moo,

And they might scare her so bad she might

    throw a shoe.

She had heard stories of cows switching their tails

And stomping so hard they'd bang up milk pails,

And trample through gardens and trample

    through fences,

And chase little girls who were left so defenseless.

So she asked her mom for some good cow advice,

And her mom just said, "Keep walking and act

    real nice.

And keep this in mind: old cows can be sly,

So never ever, ever look 'em straight in the eye.

Just keep on the road; just keep on your track,

And never ever, ever look back."

So the little girl started out with the pasture ahead,

And she thought and she thought, "Don't forget

    what Ma said.

Just keep on a-walking and walk real fast,

And before you know it, you'll be walked way past."

So the little girl started, one step then another,

And all of a sudden, there was a baby calf with

     her mother.

She was now next to all of them cows in the pasture,

So she tried to start walking faster and faster.

Then she heard one cow say, "Mmm," and

     another say, "Moo,"

But she thought they said, "We're coming for you."

She wanted to look back to see how close they were.

She bet they were so close she could reach out

     and touch fur.

She tried to keep walking; then she heard a hoof stomp.

And the next thing she heard was a big old chomp.

"I can't get chomped," she heard the words her

     mom told her.

But she did it anyway; she looked over her shoulder.

And there were all these cows standing right by

the fence.

And about right now, the little girl was a little tense.

And these cows were all staring at her with their

big round cow eyes.

And the little girl whispered, "Please let me pass,

you guys."

So she took a step, and they took a step too,

Not just one cow, but the whole cow crew.

And the little girl knew she had to look back

'Cause she knew right along they were planning

their attack.

So she peeked over her shoulder with her eyes

open sorta wide,

But the cows were chewing grass, mouths going

side to side.

Then she kinda got the feeling the cows didn't

care what she was doing

As long as...

they were content
eating grass
and just mooing.

moo

"You mean they aren't gonna jump the fence

      and stampede with their feet

Or maybe break the gate and look for little girls to eat?

Looks like they don't even care I'm walking to

      my friends,

And look, the fence and cows are coming to an end.

I'm still walking, but I'm not walking too fast,

And lookie here, I'm almost past.

Turns out cows aren't too scary," she thought

      with a grin,

"As long as there's a big ol' fence to hold 'em all in."

So that little girl walked straight to her friends,

And that's how the cows in the pasture story ends.

She knew in her heart the conflict was over.

She was chewing on gum; they were chomping

      on clover.

# RAINDROP FAMILY

# RAINDROP FAMILY

A family of raindrops lived in the sky.

They lived in a cloud way up high.

The cloud where they lived was fluffy and gray,

And they lived in that cloud day after day.

From their gray cloud home above the trees,

They could feel the warm sun and feel the cool breeze.

When the sun went down and the moon would rise,

The Raindrop family would sleep in the skies.

Then one day, Father Raindrop looked down

And saw that the earth was parched and brown.

"Family," he said, "it is time for a trip.

You see, we are rain and the earth needs a sip."

So the sun hid its face in a shadowy wrap.

As there came a great thunder, a boom and a clap.

Then lightning came out and flashed out a bolt

That sliced through the air, hitting Earth with a jolt.

All the critters on earth, upon seeing the light,

Scurried and hustled to get out of sight.

A robin looked up and ruffled a feather

While sensing a delicate change in the weather.

A lazy old turtle crept down the lane,

Stuck his head in his shell and said,

    "Here comes the rain."

Even the tiniest worm in the ground

Knew that some rain would be coming around.

Worm turned to his mother and said with a smile,

"Instead of an inch, we'll be swimming a mile."

Finally, the raindrops started to dance,

And they were joined in by their uncles and aunts.

Then cousins and nieces and nephews stepped up,

And it was time for that cloud to erupt.

WITH ANOTHER

BIG FLASH

AND A

THUNDEROUS

ROAR,

The cloud that was home finally opened its door.

The family of raindrops began their wet ride

Down to the earth that was parched and dried.

"Here we go!" cried the father, "We're fast on our way

Down to the ground from our cloud, nice and gray.

We must leave our home that we love so much;

The flowers and grass are awaiting our touch."

So one by one, like a raindrop parade,

The raindrops fell down; the storm was made.

Every aunt, every uncle were dripping their drop

Down to the earth where their journey would stop.

Each drop of water that fell from that cloud

Made each blade of grass happy and proud.

And flowers gave thanks to the cloud that did burst:

"Thank you, oh thank you for quenching our thirst."

Small animals drank from a shimmering pool,

And the air was fresh and clean and cool.

Even humans came out to give thanks to the skies

With their dancing and cheering and happiness cries.

Little girls put on their yellow rain boots,

And splashed through puddles with hollers

and hoots.

Little boys went out in their little bare feet

To walk in the water that sat in the street.

Then the winds calmed and came to a rest,

Knowing the rain had given its best.

The heavens returned to a soft shade of blue

While the earth and its gardens were growing anew.

All life on earth had returned to its glory

And that is a wonderful end to this story

Except for that rainbow that stretched clear

through space

And made the world a more beautiful place.

A beautiful place we can all live together

No matter the storm, no matter the weather!

# ACKNOWLEDGMENTS

To GBR for his patience and encouragement.

To my four amazing girls - thank you for being my personal cheer squad, technical support team and sounding board. You each helped bring this book to life.

And then - thank you to Lisa Pelto whose knowledge and care take my rough ideas and make them polished and lovely.

You help my words find their home.